Carrie's Surprise

The Sound of Hard C

by Joanne Meier and Cecilia Minden • illustrated by Bob Ostrom

The Child's World

Published by The Child's World®
1980 Lookout Drive
Mankato, MN 56003-1705
800-599-READ
www.childsworld.com

The Child's World®: Mary Berendes, Publishing Director
The Design Lab: Design and page production

Library of Congress Cataloging-in-Publication Data
Meier, Joanne D.
  Carrie's surprise : the sound of hard c / by Joanne
Meier and Cecilia Minden ; illustrated by Bob Ostrom.
     p. cm.
  ISBN 978-1-60253-395-0 (library bound : alk. paper)
  1. English language—Consonants—Juvenile literature.
2. English language—Phonetics—Juvenile literature 3.
Reading—Phonetic method—Juvenile literature. I. Minden,
Cecilia. II. Ostrom, Bob. III. Title.
  PE1159.M453 2010
  [E]—dc22   2010002909

Printed in the United States of America in Mankato, MN.
July 2010
F11538

NOTE TO PARENTS AND EDUCATORS:

The Child's World® has created this series with the goal of exposing children to engaging stories and illustrations that assist in phonics development. The books in the series will help children learn the relationships between the letters of written language and the individual sounds of spoken language. This contact helps children learn to use these relationships to read and write words.

The books in this series follow a similar format. An introductory page, to be read by an adult, introduces the child to the phonics feature, or sound, that will be highlighted in the book. Read this page to the child, stressing the phonic feature. Help the student learn how to form the sound with her mouth. The story and engaging illustrations follow the introduction. At the end of the story, word lists categorize the feature words into their phonic elements.

Each book in this series has been carefully written to meet specific readability requirements. Close attention has been paid to elements such as word count, sentence length, and vocabulary. Readability formulas measure the ease with which the text can be read and understood. Each book in this series has been analyzed using the Spache readability formula.

Reading research suggests that systematic phonics instruction can greatly improve students' word recognition, spelling, and comprehension skills. This series assists in the teaching of phonics by providing students with important opportunities to apply their knowledge of phonics as they read words, sentences, and text.

The letter c makes two sounds.

The soft sound of **c** sounds like **c** as in: *celery* and *centipede*.

The hard sound of **c** sounds like **c** as in: *cap* and *coat*.

In this book, you will read words that have the hard **c** sound as in: *cat, card, cake,* and *color*.

Today is a big day
for Carrie.

It is Mother's birthday.

Carrie will make a cake.

She will make a card.

Carrie puts cold milk in the bowl. She adds the egg. She stirs and stirs. Father puts everything else in the bowl.

"Now the cake must cook,"
says Father.

"Be careful!" says Carrie.

Carrie makes a card.

She colors a cow.

She colors a cat, just like

their pet.

Father puts the card and cake on the table.

"Mother will be so surprised! Let's give them to her now!" says Carrie.

Mother could not believe her eyes! "How nice!" says Mother. "I did not know you could cook like this."

Mother cut everyone a big piece of cake. Even the cat!

Fun Facts

You probably enjoy cake. Did you know that many people believe this tasty dessert can bring good luck? On your birthday, your friends might tell you to make a wish before blowing out the candles on your cake. If you don't tell anyone your wish, some people think it may come true! When two people get married, they often save part of their wedding cake and then eat it one year later. This also is supposed to bring good luck.

Think cooking is easy? Imagine if you had to cook a 75-pound (34-kilogram) turkey for Thanksgiving dinner! This was one of the largest turkeys ever produced. It took almost 19 hours to cook.

Activity

Baking a Cake

Talk to your parents about baking a cake together. You could use a recipe someone else made up, or you could even write one of your own! Discuss what ingredients you plan to use. Make sure you have all of them handy before you begin baking. When you are done, let the cake cool. Then add frosting or sprinkles. Most importantly, don't forget to share the cake with your friends and family!

To Learn More

Books
About the Sound of Hard C
Moncure, Jane Belk. *My "c" Sound Box®*. Mankato, MN: The Child's World, 2009.

About Cakes
Elya, Susan Middleton, and Lee Chapman (illustrator). *Eight Animals Bake a Cake*. New York: G. P. Putnam's Sons, 2002.

London, Jonathan, and Frank Remkiewicz (illustrator). *Froggy Bakes a Cake*. New York: Grosset & Dunlap, 2000.

Rylant, Cynthia, and Arthur Howard (illustrator). *Mr. Putter and Tabby Bake the Cake*. San Diego: Harcourt Brace, 1994.

About Baking
Bull, Jane. *The Baking Book*. New York: Dorling Kindersley, 2005.

Cole, Joanna, and Ted Enik (illustrator). *The Magic School Bus Gets Baked in a Cake: A Book About Kitchen Chemistry*. New York: Scholastic, 1995.

Dodge, Abigail Johnson. *Kids Baking*. Menlo Park, CA: Oxmoor House, 2003.

Web Sites
Visit our home page for lots of links about the Sound of Hard C:

childsworld.com/links

Note to Parents, Teachers, and Librarians: We routinely check our Web links to make sure they're safe, active sites—so encourage your readers to check them out!

Hard C
Feature Words

Proper Names
Carrie

Feature Words in Initial Position
cake
card
careful
cat
cold
color
cook
could
cow
cut

About the Authors

Joanne Meier, PhD, has worked as an elementary school teacher, university professor, and researcher. She earned her BA in early childhood education from the University of South Carolina, and her MEd and PhD in education from the University of Virginia. She currently works as a literacy consultant for schools and private organizations. Joanne lives in Virginia with her husband Eric, daughters Kella and Erin, two cats, and a gerbil.

Cecilia Minden, PhD, is the former director of the Language and Literacy Program at the Harvard Graduate School of Education. She is now a reading consultant for school and library publications. She earned her PhD in reading education from the University of Virginia. Cecilia and her husband, Dave Cupp, live outside Chapel Hill, North Carolina. They enjoy sharing their love of reading with their grandchildren, Chelsea and Qadir.

About the Illustrator

Bob Ostrom has been illustrating children's books for nearly twenty years. A graduate of the New England School of Art & Design at Suffolk University, Bob has worked for such companies as Disney, Nickelodeon, and Cartoon Network. He lives in North Carolina with his wife Melissa and three children, Will, Charlie, and Mae.